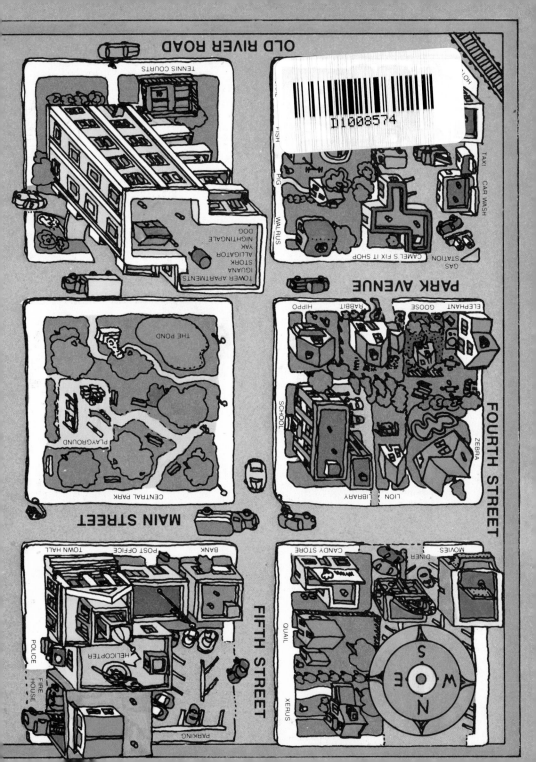

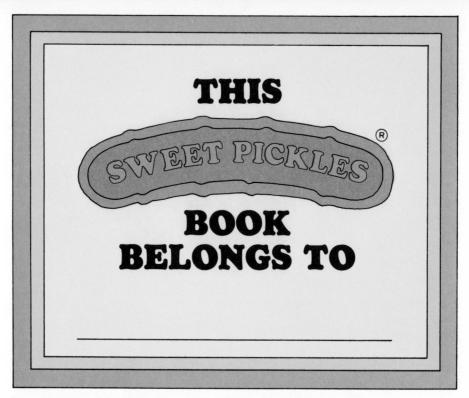

THIS

SWEET PICKLES ®

BOOK BELONGS TO

_____

In the world of *Sweet Pickles,* each animal gets into a pickle because of an all too human personality trait.

This book is about Loving Lion who would like to love everybody all of the time.

Other Books in the Sweet Pickles Series

WHO STOLE ALLIGATOR'S SHOE?
FIXED BY CAMEL
ELEPHANT EATS THE PROFITS
GOOSE GOOFS OFF
ME TOO IGUANA
MOODY MOOSE BUTTONS
QUAIL CAN'T DECIDE
STORK SPILLS THE BEANS
VERY WORRIED WALRUS
YAKETY YAK YAK YAK
ZIP GOES ZEBRA

Library of Congress Cataloging in Publication Data

Hefter, Richard.
  Lion is down in the dumps.

  (Sweet Pickles series)
  SUMMARY: Lion figures out a scheme to have his
roller skates and lend them, too.
  [1. Lions—Fiction] I. Title. II. Series.
PZ7.H3587Li   [E]   77-7256
ISBN 0-03-021441-6

Printed in the United States of America

Weekly Reader Books' Edition

Weekly Reader Books presents

LION
IS DOWN IN
THE DUMPS

Written and Illustrated
by Richard Hefter
Edited by Ruth Lerner Perle

Holt, Rinehart and Winston · New York

"Enough!" mumbled Lion, as he walked slowly down the street. "I've had just about enough!"

"Morning, Lion," called Camel. "Where are you going so early?"

"I know you're supposed to love your friends," muttered Lion, "but this is too much!"

"What are you talking about?" asked Camel.

"Borrowing..." cried Lion, "...and not feeling friendly...and my new skates!"

"If your skates are broken," said Camel, "I can fix them."

It's not my skates," sobbed Lion. "It's my heart!" Lion trudged off slowly down the street.

Lion walked right past Hippo and didn't even say hello.

He marched past Rabbit and didn't say good morning.

Yak pulled his taxi over to the curb and tried to talk to Lion, but Lion kept right on walking.

Camel stopped Hippo. "Hippo," she said, "Lion seems awfully sad. Did he say anything to you?"

"No," answered Hippo. "He didn't even say hello."

"He didn't say good morning to me, either," said Rabbit. "And that's not like him. Lion is usually so friendly."

"Lion is upset and down in the dumps!" called Yak, as he drove by in his taxi.

"We know that," shouted Hippo. "But *why* is he down in the dumps?"

"Don't know," said Yak, and he drove away.

"I wonder what's wrong with him," said Hippo.

"Well," said Camel, "he *did* say something about not feeling friendly."

"But Lion is always friendly," cried Rabbit. "He has more friends than anyone in town."

"He also said something about borrowing," said Camel. "Has anyone borrowed anything from Lion lately?"

Rabbit scratched his head. "As a matter of fact, I borrowed his garden hose last Wednesday. But I'm not due to return it until Friday, at 4:20 P.M."

"I borrowed his bicycle," puffed Hippo, "but I was going to return it this afternoon."

Camel thought a moment. "I still have the hammer I borrowed from him when I was fixing his roof!"

"Maybe that's it," said Hippo. "Maybe Lion's upset because everybody has been borrowing his stuff."

"In that case," said Rabbit, "let's get everybody to return his stuff!"

"That should fix things!" agreed Camel.

They walked all around town.

Alligator had Lion's umbrella. She said it was Lion's fault because it rained the last time she visited him and she had to borrow it.

Goose thought that she might have borrowed some crayons from Lion, but she couldn't find them. So she decided to return some cookies instead.

Walrus had Lion's red woolly hat and a pair of green mittens.

Vulture had Lion's mirror.

Elephant had Lion's picnic basket.

Octopus had four pairs of Lion's socks.

Quail wasn't sure.

Nightingale didn't care.

Kangaroo said, "I took his marbles and two golf balls and a toy truck, but I was only kidding."

Everywhere they stopped, someone had borrowed something from Lion.

"Now," said Camel, "let's take all this stuff back to Lion. That will cheer him up."

Everybody marched over to Lion's house.
He wasn't home.

"Where could he be?" wondered Quail.
"Now I'm really worried," moaned Walrus. "This is serious!"
"I told you," shouted Yak from his taxi. "Lion is down in the dumps."

"We know that," yelled Alligator. "But *where* is he?"

"Why doesn't anyone ever listen around here?" screamed Yak. "When I say Lion is down in the dumps, I mean it. HE IS DOWN IN THE DUMPS! I don't understand you guys. I followed Lion in my taxi, and he was going down to the town dumps. So I told you where he was, and that he didn't look very happy to me, and that the town dumps is no place for someone who isn't happy and…hey… where are you going?"

Everybody rushed to the town dumps. And there was
Lion, carrying a box.

"Lion, Lion!" shouted Camel. "Everything's fixed now!"

"What are you talking about?" asked Lion.

"We brought back all the things we borrowed from you," said Camel. "We thought that would cheer you up."

"But, Camel," said Lion, with a little tear in his eye, "I don't need all that stuff back. That's not why I'm unhappy."

"Well, what is it then?" asked Hippo.

Another tear slid down Lion's face. "It's my new roller skates!"

"Your new roller skates?" asked Camel.

"Yes," said Lion. "I don't want to lend my new skates, and I *know* one of you will want to borrow them. And if I say no, I'll feel mean and unfriendly. And I don't like to feel that way!"

"So," said Lion, "I came down here to the dumps to find a couple of boxes and some wood."

"Why?" asked Quail.

"Because," said Lion, "if I build two scooters with boxes and wood, and I use one roller skate for the wheels on each scooter, then I have one scooter to ride on, and one to lend to my friends. That way, I can make everybody happy."

"Are you sure?" asked Quail.

Then everyone helped Lion build two scooters.
When they were finished, Lion smiled and said,
"Thanks a lot, guys. Now, who would like the
first ride?"

I would!" shouted Alligator, and she hopped on one of the scooters and took off down the street.

"Me too!" yelled Iguana. And she hopped on the other scooter and rode away.

Lion scratched his mane. "Gee," he sighed. "I think something went wrong."

"I guess you should have built three scooters!" snickered Kangaroo.